WHEN DAD TRAVELS FOR WORK

KRISTOPHER JAMES GOEDEN

Illustrated by CSILLA SZEGEDI

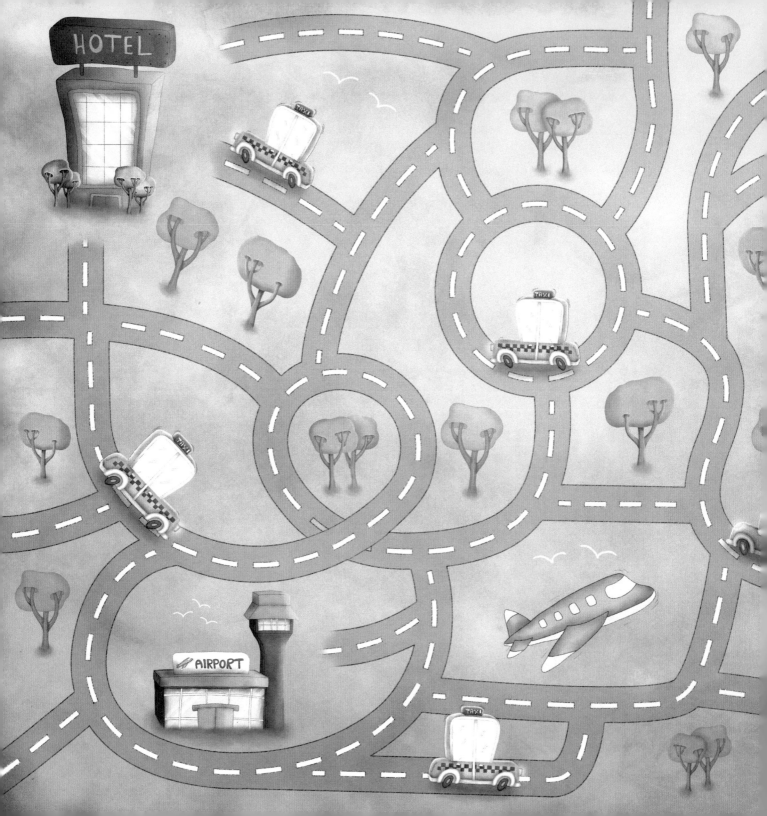

For Krew and Slater: There's nowhere else in the world I'd rather be than with you boys. Love, Dad

Publisher's Cataloguing-in-Publication Data
Names: Goeden, Kristopher, author. | Szegedi, Csilla, illustrator.
Title: When Dad Travels for Work / by Kristopher James Goeden ; illustrated by Csilla Szegedi
Description: First edition. | Urbandale, IA ; Unless Ventures [2023] | Summary: This story told in rhyming text explains to children why a dad may need to leave home for work and what they can do to help the family while that parent is away.
Identifiers: LCCN 2022917437 | ISBN 979-8-9869406-3-2 (hc) | ISBN 979-8-9869406-0-1 (paperback) | ISBN 979-8-9869406-6-3 (ebook)
Subjects: | CYAC: Stories in rhyme - Fiction | Family life - Fiction | Travel - Fiction | Schools - Fiction | Work and family - Fiction.
Classification: LCC PZ8.3.G64346 Whe 2023 | DDC [E] - dc23

Book design and Illustrations by Csilla Szegedi

Printed in the United States

First Edition

Published by Unless Ventures
Urbandale, IA
www.UnlessVenturesLLC.com

WHEN DAD TRAVELS
FOR WORK

KRISTOPHER JAMES GOEDEN
Illustrated by CSILLA SZEGEDI

Before you woke up,
Dad had to be gone.

He whispered goodbye as he left

BEFORE DAWN.

Dad needs to travel and work
FAR AWAY,

while you stay at home and begin your
NEW DAY.

When you were at school, he soared up above.

No matter the distance, he sends you his **LOVE.**

While Daddy's away, he'll be sure to **WORK HARD.**

He hopes you'll have fun
PLAYING GAMES
in the yard.

Dad goes to work to make money, you see,

to buy things we need –
SINCE FOOD ISN'T FREE.

While Dad's off at work, we all must pitch in.
Completing your chores would be
A BIG WIN!

When Dad's not at home,
please keep in mind

to be helpful, supportive,

AND MOST OF ALL, KIND.

Each night in your dreams,
Dad hopes that you'll roam,

then share your adventures
WHEN HE RETURNS HOME.

Dad may have to travel and work quite a lot,

but smile and know
**FAMILY'S HIS ONE
FAVORITE THOUGHT.**

And once he comes back,
he wants, far and above,

to care for his family with
ALL OF HIS LOVE.

DADDY
LOVES YOU.

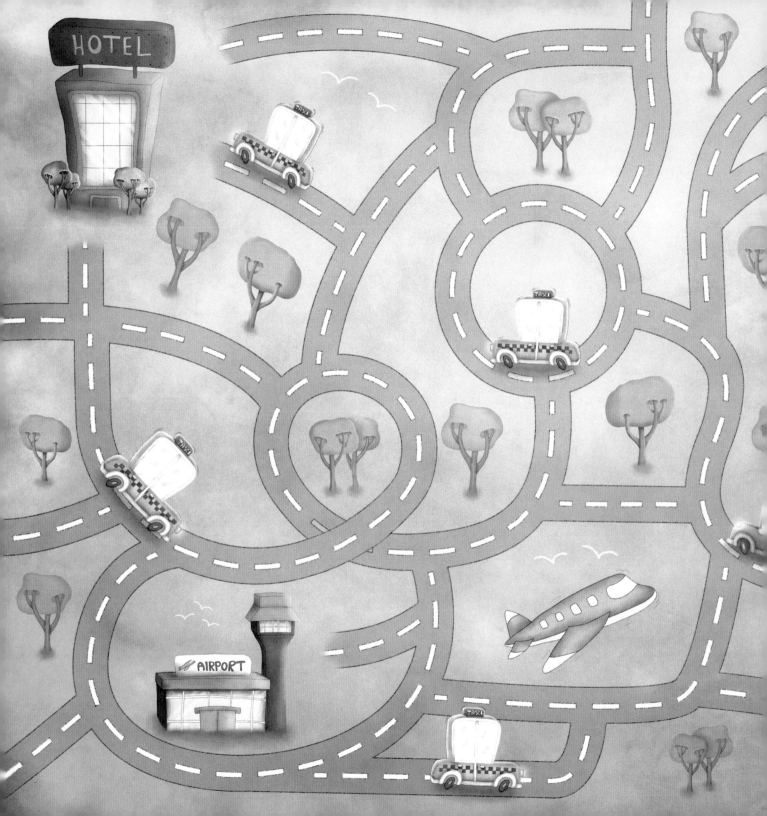

Made in the USA
Monee, IL
01 November 2024

69024986R10021